5/23

Dear Parents:

Congratulations! Your child is taking the first steps on an exciting journey. The destination? Independent reading!

STEP INTO READING® will help your child get there. The program offers five steps to reading success. Each step includes fun stories and colorful art or photographs. In addition to original fiction and books with favorite characters, there are Step into Reading Non-Fiction Readers, Phonics Readers and Boxed Sets, Sticker Readers, and Comic Readers—a complete literacy program with something to interest every child.

Learning to Read, Step by Step!

Ready to Read   Preschool–Kindergarten
• big type and easy words • rhyme and rhythm • picture clues
For children who know the alphabet and are eager to begin reading.

Reading with Help   Preschool–Grade 1
• basic vocabulary • short sentences • simple stories
For children who recognize familiar words and sound out new words with help.

Reading on Your Own   Grades 1–3
• engaging characters • easy-to-follow plots • popular topics
For children who are ready to read on their own.

Reading Paragraphs   Grades 2–3
• challenging vocabulary • short paragraphs • exciting stories
For newly independent readers who read simple sentences with confidence.

Ready for Chapters   Grades 2–4
• chapters • longer paragraphs • full-color art
For children who want to take the plunge into chapter books but still like colorful pictures.

STEP INTO READING® is designed to give every child a successful reading experience. The grade levels are only guides; children will progress through the steps at their own speed, developing confidence in their reading.

Remember, a lifetime love of reading starts with a single step!

Copyright © 2023 Disney Enterprises, Inc. and Pixar. All rights reserved. Published in the United States by Random House Children's Books, a division of Penguin Random House LLC, 1745 Broadway, New York, NY 10019, and in Canada by Penguin Random House Canada Limited, Toronto, in conjunction with Disney Enterprises, Inc.

Step into Reading, Random House, and the Random House colophon are registered trademarks of Penguin Random House LLC.

Visit us on the Web!
StepIntoReading.com
rhcbooks.com

Educators and librarians, for a variety of teaching tools, visit us at RHTeachersLibrarians.com

ISBN 978-0-7364-4373-9 (trade) — ISBN 978-0-7364-9038-2 (lib. bdg.)
ISBN 978-0-7364-4374-6 (ebook)

Printed in the United States of America   10 9 8 7 6 5 4 3 2 1

STEP INTO READING®

DISNEY · PIXAR

ELEMENTAL

Better Together

adapted by Kathy McCullough

illustrated by the Disney Storybook Art Team

Random House 🏠 New York

Welcome to Element City!
Fire, Water, Earth
and Air people live
here as neighbors.

Bernie and Cinder
are Fire people.
They moved to the city
to start a new life.

Ember is Bernie
and Cinder's daughter.
Her flame burns bright!

Ember can use her
heat to shape sand
into pretty glass.

Ember works in
her parents' shop.
She wants to make
them proud.

When Ember is upset,
her fire changes.
Whenever she gets angry,
she explodes!

This is Wade.

He is a Water person

who lives in

the Water District.

Wade cries when
he is happy.
He cries when
he is sad.

This is Clod.

He is an Earth person.

Earth people can grow

plants on their bodies!

Fern is also
an Earth person.
He works at City Hall.

Gale is an Air person.
Air people can float—
and even fly!

Lutz plays airball.

Airball is a fun game!

Wade visits Ember.

He eats some kol nuts.

The nuts are too hot

for a Water person!

Ember is not sure
that different Elements
can be friends.

But Wade wants
to be Ember's friend.
He takes her
to Mineral Lake.
He shows her how
he can make a rainbow.
Ember's flame changes.

Wade and Ember see that amazing things happen when different Elements come together.

They learn to trust
each other.

Ember and Wade

become friends!

Element City is
a place for everyone!